DREAMS of GLORY

DREAMS OF GLORY

poems starring girls

★ selected by Isabel Joshlin Glaser ★

with illustrations by Pat Lowery Collins

ATHENEUM BOOKS FOR YOUNG READERS

For little girls and big girls.

For all girls everywhere.

For Barbara and for Marcia who said, YES.

A Lucas/Evans Book

Text Copyright © 1995 by Isabel Joshlin Glaser
Illustrations copyright © 1995 by Pat Lowery Collins

Atheneum Books for Young Readers
An imprint of Simon & Schuster Children's Publishing Division
1230 Avenue of the Americas
New York, NY 10020

The text of this book is set in 12 pt. Zapf Book Light.

First edition

Printed in the United States of America

10   9   8   7   6   5   4   3   2   1

Library of Congress Cataloging-in-Publication Data

Dreams of glory : poems starring girls / selected by Isabel Joshlin Glaser ;
    illustrated by Pat Lowery Collins.
        p.   cm.
    ISBN 0-689-31891-X (cl.)
    1.Girls—Juvenile poetry. 2. Children's poetry, American.
I. Glaser, Isabel Joshlin. II. Collins, Pat Lowery.
PS595.G47D73   1995   95-15302
811.008'0352042—dc20   CIP
                                                          AC

ACKNOWLEDGMENTS

Every effort has been made to trace the ownership of all copyrighted material and to secure the necessary permissions to reprint these selections. In the event of any question as to the use of any material the editor and the publisher, while expressing regret for any inadvertent error, will be happy to make the necessary correction in future printings.

Grateful acknowledgment is made to the following for permission to reprint the copyrighted material listed below.

ADDISON-WESLEY PUBLISHING COMPANY, INC., for "I Am Rose" from *The World is Round* by Gertrude Stein. Copyright © 1966 by Addison-Wesley Publishing Company, Inc. Reprinted with permission of the publisher.

ATHENEUM PUBLISHERS, for "At the Horse Show" from *A Grass Green Gallop* by Patricia Hubbell. Copyright © 1990 by Patricia Hubbel. Reprinted with permission of Atheneum Publishers, an imprint of Macmillan Publishing Company.

ANN R. BLAKESLEE, for "The Dare"; "Dreams of Glory," reprinted from CRICKET, March 1990. Copyright © 1990 by Ann R. Blakeslee. Both poems used by permission of the author, who controls all rights.

BRADBURY PRESS, for "The Rescue" from *Waiting to Waltz* by Cynthia Rylant. Copyright © 1984 by Cynthia Rylant. Reprinted with permission of Bradbury Press, an Affiliate of Macmillan, Inc.

CURTIS BROWN, LTD., for "Girls Can, Too!" from *Girls Can Too!* by Lee Bennett Hopkins. Copyright © 1972 by Lee Bennet Hopkins. Reprinted by permission of Curtis Brown, Ltd.

CLARION BOOKS/HOUGHTON MIFFLIN CO., for "Darcy Tanner" from *Class Dismissed* by Mel Glenn. Text copyright © 1982 by Mel Glenn; "Crystal Rowe (Track Star)" from *Class Dismissed II* by Mel Glenn. Text copyright © 1986 by Mel Glenn. Both poems used by permission of Clarion Books/Houghton Mifflin Co. All rights reserved.

DUTTON CHILDREN'S BOOKS, for "Where's Mary?" from *Fairies and Suchlike* by Ivy O. Eastwick. Copyright © 1946 by E. P. Dutton & Co., Inc., renewed © 1974 by Ivy Olive Eastwick. Used by permission of Dutton Children's Books, a division of Penguin Books USA Inc.

FARRAR, STRAUS & GIROUX, INC., for "mattie lou at twelve" from *Spin a Soft Black Song* by Nikki Giovanni. Copyright © 1971, 1985 by Nikki Giovanni. Reprinted by permission of Farrar, Straus & Giroux, Inc.

ISABEL JOSHLIN GLASER, for "At the Pool" and "Basket-Blasting"; "Prediction: School P. E.," reprinted from *Cricket*, April 1990. Copyright © 1990 by Isabel Joshlin Glaser. All rights are controlled by the author.

HARPERCOLLINS, for "Narcissa" from *Bronzeville Boys and Girls* by Gwendolyn Brooks. Copyright © 1956 by Gwendolyn Brooks Blakely; "So I'm Proud" from *Hey World, Here I Am!* by Jean Little. Copyright © 1986 by Jean Little. Both poems reprinted by permission of HarperCollins Publishers.

Contents

SPORTS

GIRLS CAN, TOO!   Lee Bennett Hopkins   11

THE DARE   Ann R. Blakeslee   12

SKIING   Rose Burgunder   13

74TH STREET   Myra Cohn Livingston   14

ICE SKATING   Sandra Liatsos   15

PREDICTION: SCHOOL P.E.   Isabel Joshlin Glaser   16

AT THE HORSE SHOW   Patricia Hubbell   17

AT THE POOL   Isabel Joshlin Glaser   18

CRYSTAL ROWE (Track Star)   Mel Glenn   19

THE FINISH LINE   Lillian Morrison   20

POWER

I AM ROSE   Gertrude Stein   23

I'M GOING TO PET A WORM TODAY   Constance Levy   24

THE RESCUE   Cynthia Rylant   25

HE MAKES ME SO MAD   John Ridland   26

ALL I DID WAS ASK MY SISTER A QUESTION   John Ciardi   27

ABIGAIL   Kaye Starbird   28

DARCY TANNER   Mel Glenn   30

NIGHT PRACTICE   May Swenson   31

SO I'M PROUD   Jean Little   32

mattie lou at twelve   Nikki Giovanni   33

THE FROG PRINCESS   Gwen Strauss   34

DREAMS OF GLORY

TO DARK EYES DREAMING   Zilpha Keatley Snyder   39

WHERE'S MARY?   Ivy O. Eastwick   40

THEY'RE CALLING   Felice Holman   41

PRIVATE TIME   Bobbi Katz   42

NARCISSA   Gwendolyn Brooks   43

DREAMS OF GLORY   Ann R. Blakeslee   44

BASKET-BLASTING   Isabel Joshlin Glaser   45

JAIME'S WISH   Cynthia S. Pederson   46

THUMBPRINT   Eve Merriam   47

Sports

. . . Well, girls can, too!

GIRLS CAN, TOO!

Tony said: "Boys are better!
  They can . . .
    whack a ball,
    ride a bike with one hand,
    leap off a wall."

I just listened
  and when he was through,
I laughed and said:

  "Oh, yeah! Well, girls can, too!"

Then I leaped off the wall
  and rode away
With his 200 baseball cards
  I won that day.

LEE BENNETT HOPKINS

THE DARE

Come walk the alley fence
Come tight-rope like a clown
Before Dad sees we're up too high
And shouts to get us down.

As confident as cats
We'll glide across the top
Hoping Mom doesn't look outside
And order us to stop.

We'll maybe lose our nerve
We'll maybe crash and fall
They'll probably shake their heads and say
"This doesn't make a bit of sense!
We warned you girls just yesterday."
And send you home and make me stay.
But still—I dare you anyway,
To walk the alley fence.

ANN R. BLAKESLEE

SKIING

Fast as foxes,
buzzy as bees
down the slope
on our silver-tipped skis—

early in the morning
Roseanna and I
far from our house
on the hilltop fly.

A snowbird's yawning,
the sky's all pink,
somewhere in the valley
the lights still blink.

No one's awake
but us, and a bird.
The day's too beautiful
to speak a word.

ROSE BURGUNDER

74TH STREET

Hey, this little kid gets roller skates.
She puts them on.
She stands up and almost
flops over backwards.
She sticks out a foot like
she's going somewhere and
falls down and
smacks her hand. She
grabs hold of a step to get up and
sticks out the other foot and
slides about six inches and
falls and
skins her knee.

        And then, you know what?

She brushes off the dirt and the
blood and puts some
spit on it and then
sticks out the other foot

        again.

MYRA COHN LIVINGSTON

ICE SKATING

Higher and higher
I glide in the sky,
My feet flashing silver,
A star in each eye.
With wind at my back
I can float, I can soar.
The earth cannot hold me
In place anymore.

SANDRA LIATSOS

PREDICTION: SCHOOL P.E.

Someday
when the baseball's
   hurtling
like some UFO,
   blazing
like some mad thing
   toward me
      in outfield,
I *won't* gasp
and dodge. Oh, no!
Instead, I'll be
calmer than Calm
   —so la-de-da!—
I'll just reach out
   like a *pro*
and catch it and—quick!—
   throw to second.
And everyone will say, "Hooray!
Natalie made a double play!"
Some day.

ISABEL JOSHLIN GLASER

16

AT THE HORSE SHOW

Jennifer Rose,
  on her big dun horse,
  gallops the local hunter course.
Jennifer's horse, "The Paddock's Pride,"
  takes the in-and-out in his stride.
  He clears the hedge. He clears the stile.
  He gallops gaily the full half mile.
He's a lop-eared dun with a Roman nose,
But—"Looks aren't *all*," says Jennifer Rose.
The judges mark their books and smile.
They pin the blue to his gleaming bridle.
Jennifer rubs his homely nose—
  "He's a lovely horse," says Jennifer Rose.

PATRICIA HUBBELL

AT THE POOL

Spotlighted by the sun,
she walks to the end
    of the board
in view of everyone
and pauses, thinking:
    Some day ... the Olympics?
A bounce—nice balance!—
and she's off ...
    sails up and up
to heights of blue unleapt before.
And then, with perfect timing,
    at the apex of this airy climbing
        Marie somersaults!
        arcing gracefully down
in a trim-nutbrown-triple spiraling-OOPS!
sprawling-crashing-bashing-splashing-
        bellyflop-of-a-dive!
But she surfaces with a smile
that warms the silent shiverers
        and someone applauds
        and someone whistles
        and she thinks: *Yes*!
the last minute of the last day of the swimming season.

ISABEL JOSHLIN GLASER

CRYSTAL ROWE
(Track Star)

Allthegirlsarebunched
togetheratthestarting
_____line_____

But

When the gun goes off

I

J

U

M

P

out ahead and
never look back
and
HIT
the

__T__A__P__E__

a
WINNER!

MEL GLENN

THE FINISH LINE

There is the finish line
but the runner can cross it
again and again.

She will not be finished
for a long time
but always beginning

getting ready and set
for another GO!
a better finish.

LILLIAN MORRISON

Power

. . . and she would smile and go her way
because she knew

I AM ROSE

I am Rose my eyes are blue
I am Rose and who are you?
I am Rose and when I sing
I am Rose like anything.

GERTRUDE STEIN

I'M GOING TO PET A WORM TODAY

I'm going to pet a worm today.
I'm going to pet a worm. Don't say,
"Don't pet a worm"—I'm doing it soon.
Emily's coming this afternoon!
And you know what she'll probably say:
"I touched a mouse," or
"I held a snake," or
"I felt a dead bird's wing."
And she'll turn to me with a kind of smile.
"What did you do that's interesting?"
This time
I am
Going to say,
"Why, Emily, you should have seen me
Pet a worm today!"
And I'll tell her he shrank and he stretched like elastic,
And I got a chill and it felt fantastic.
And I'll watch her smile
Fade away when she
Wishes, that moment,
That she could be me!

CONSTANCE LEVY

24

THE RESCUE

Running down the tracks one day,
thunder and lightning coming up on me,
and there a little girl crying
and walking,
looking at the sky.
Me scared to death of storms
crossing over:
You going home? Want me to walk with you?
And turning away from my house to walk her
through Beaver
to hers.
Lightning and thunder strong now.
So there's her mother on the porch, waving,
and she says bye to me then runs.
I turn around
and walk in the storm
slow and straight,
but inside,
a little girl crying.

CYNTHIA RYLANT

HE MAKES ME SO MAD

I nail my
little brother
with a stare

where he sits
at the counter
giving me

his smart mouth
while I boil my
egg. Beyond

him, Father
simmers in his
easy chair,

our four heads
lining up: Dad,
daughter, son,

and hard-boiled
egg hot-headed
it its cup.

JOHN RIDLAND

ALL I DID WAS ASK MY SISTER A QUESTION

Why is water wet? Let's see—
Because . . . Well, silly, it has to be!
How could you drink it if it were dry?
If you got a drop of it in your eye
It would sting like sand and make you cry.
When it started to rain, it would come down dust.
You'd have to hold your breath till you bust
Or turn to powder inside your chest.
And how would I pass my swimming test
And get my badge? Not that you'd care.
You'd still be standing around somewhere
Asking foolish questions to get me mad!
Well, I'll tell Mother and she'll tell Dad.
Then see what he does to you for that!
And see if I care, you little brat!

JOHN CIARDI

ABIGAIL

Abigail knew when she was born
Among the roses, she was a thorn.
Her quiet mother had lovely looks.
Her quiet father wrote quiet books.
Her quiet brothers, correct though pale,
Weren't really prepared for Abigail
Who entered the house with howls and tears
While both of her brothers blocked their ears
And both of her parents, talking low,
Said, "Why is Abigail screaming so?"

Abigail kept on getting worse.
As soon as she teethed she bit her nurse.
At three, she acted distinctly cool
Toward people and things at nursery school.
"I'm sick of cutting out dolls," she said,
And cut a hole in her dress, instead.
Her mother murmured, "She's bold for three."
Her father answered, "I quite agree."
Her brothers mumbled, "We hate to fuss,
But *when* will Abigail be like us?"

Abigail, going through her teens,
Liked overalls and pets and machines.
In college, hating most of its features,
She told off all of her friends and teachers.
Her brothers, graduating from Yale,
Said: "Really, you're hopeless, Abigail."
And while her mother said,"Fix your looks,"
Her father added, "Or else write books."
And Abigail asked, "Is that a dare?"
And wrote a book that would curl your hair....

KAYE STARBIRD

DARCY
TANNER

When I told my mother she didn't look well,
Could I get her something, she said,
"Stop stalling and practice your piano."
I told her I wanted to go out and play baseball.
"Nonsense," she said, "girls don't play baseball,
They play sonatas."
When I told my mother she'd get well soon,
Did she want her pills, she said,
"Stop stalling and practice your piano."
I told her there was nothing cheerful I could play.
"Nonsense," she said, "look in your collection and
    find something."
When my mother died
I stopped stalling and practiced my piano.
I spend my time now going through my collection
And playing those minor chords over and over again.

MEL GLENN

NIGHT PRACTICE

I
will
remember
with my breath
to make a mountain,
with my sucked-in breath
a valley, with my pushed-out
breath a mountain. I will make
a valley wider than the whisper, I
will make a higher mountain than the cry,
will with my will breathe a mountain, I will
with my will breathe a valley. I will push out
a mountain, suck in a valley, deeper than the shout
YOU MUST DIE, harder, heavier, sharper a mountain than
the truth YOU MUST DIE. I will remember. My breath will
make a mountain. My will will remember to will. I, suck-
ing, pushing, I will breathe a valley, I will breathe a mountain.

MAY SWENSON

SO I'M PROUD

Our History teacher says, "Be proud you're Canadians."
My father says, "You can be proud you're Jewish."
My mother says, "Stand up straight, Kate.
    Be proud you're tall."

So I'm proud.

But what I want to know is
When did I have the chance to be
    Norwegian or Buddhist or short?

JEAN LITTLE

mattie lou at twelve

they always said "what a pretty girl you are"
and she would smile

they always said "how nice of you to help
your mother with your brothers and sisters"
and she would smile and think

they said "what lovely pigtails you have
and you plaited them all by yourself!"
and she would say "thank you"

and they always said "all those B's
what a good student you are"
and she would smile and say thank you

they said "you will make a fine woman some
    day"
and she would smile and go her way

because she knew

NIKKI GIOVANNI

THE FROG PRINCESS

I always hated them,
all jump and slime.
The boy next door used to frighten me
with them behind the pool, his palms
cupping something wet and green.

Years later he said he did it all for love;
but I was a Princess then,
wanting nothing more to do with him.
So I wasn't myself
when I made that promise.

I was playing in the garden with my golden ball
Father brought back from his Crusades.
There is a deep well
I sometimes call my name down
to listen to the echo back
and back until I, too, feel hollow.

When I lost my ball, one of them,
bumpy, all eyes and mouth,
heard me or my tears shudder back.
What could I do? I was only a girl,
a Princess, but a girl—so I promised.

It arrived at dinner
lurching its way towards me.
I ordered a halt to its charade,
how dare a frog behave this way.
That's when Father betrayed me.

The meal was endless.
The slurping, burping, warty fellow
drank my royal nectar.

I thought only of escape
to my chamber, my mirror, my bed.
Then the final insult came:
the thing announced it would sleep
with me upon my goose down pillow
and Father nodded, with a distant look.

Three weeks
the puffed up thing
slept beside me.
I dared not move
or even breathe.
In the dark, I watched it
pant, a hollow smudge
on my pillow.

At last I slept and when I woke
my hand touched him.
Shock, then rage
got me hurling him
towards a wall; that's how I got
my Prince to explode from a frog.

GWEN STRAUSS

Dreams of Glory

. . . Soon she is a singing wind.
And, next, a nightingale.

TO DARK EYES DREAMING

Dreams go fast and far
 these days.
They go by rocket thrust.
They go arrayed
 in lights
  or in the dust of stars.
Dreams, these days,
 go fast and far.
Dreams are young, these days,
 or very old,
They can be black,
 or blue or gold.
They need no special charts,
 nor any fuel.
It seems, only one rule applies,
 to all our dreams—
They will not fly except in open sky.
 A fenced-in dream
  will die.

ZILPHA KEATLEY SNYDER

WHERE'S MARY?

Is Mary in the dairy?
Is Mary on the stair?
What? Mary's in the garden?
What is she doing there?
Has she made the butter yet?
Has she made the beds?
Has she topped the gooseberries
And taken off their heads?
Has she the potatoes peeled?
Has she done the grate?
Are the new green peas all shelled?
It is getting late!
What? She hasn't done a thing?
Here's a nice to-do!
Mary has a dozen jobs
And hasn't finished two.
Well! here IS a nice to-do!
Well! upon my word!
She's sitting on the garden bench
Listening to a bird!

IVY O. EASTWICK

THEY'RE CALLING

They're calling, "Nan,
Come at once."
But I don't answer.
             It's not that I don't hear,
             I'm very sharp of ear,
But I'm not Nan,
I'm a dancer.

They're calling, "Nan,
Go and wash."
But I don't go yet.
             Their voices are quite clear,
             I'm humming but I hear,
But I'm not Nan,
I'm a poet.

They're calling, "Nan,
Come to dinner!"
And I stop humming.
             I seem to hear them clearer,
             Now that dinner's nearer.
Well, just for now I'm Nan,
And I say, "Coming."

FELICE HOLMAN

PRIVATE TIME

When I'm a mom, we will have private time—
my little girl and me.
First she'll get out blue coffee cups.
(I'll put mostly milk in hers.)
Then I will listen,
really listen,
to how things were for her in school.
And I'll tell her how things were for me
down among the fishes—
down
      down
           deep in the sea,
where I'm an oceanographer.

If the phone rings
we won't answer
because it's private time.
Private for my little girl
and me.

BOBBI KATZ

NARCISSA

Some of the girls are playing jacks.
Some are playing ball.
But small Narcissa is not playing
Anything at all.

Small Narcissa sits upon
A brick in her back yard
And looks at tiger-lilies,
And shakes her pigtails hard.

First she is an ancient queen
In pomp and purple veil.
Soon she is a singing wind.
And, next, a nightingale.

How fine to be Narcissa,
A-changing like all that!
While sitting still, as still, as still
As anyone ever sat!

GWENDOLYN BROOKS

DREAMS OF GLORY

When I grow up to woman size
I think I'll be a plumber;
While snows abide
I'll work inside
And outside in the summer.
I'll have tatoos up both my arms
And swear like guttersnipes,
I'll find the rings
And other things
You lose down in your pipes.

And when I'm tired of tools and muck
I'll change and be a lady;
I'll settle down
In some nice town—
But not before I'm eighty.

ANN R. BLAKESLEE

BASKET-BLASTING

A fast leap
And she leaves the court,
Slicing through space
Like a rocket moonbound,
Motors firing her feet.
She's leaning, curving, letting go,
Whamming the ball through
So the hoop rattles
Like it's storm-sick.
And her teeth ache
And the hairs on her arms
Rise antennae-straight
And her skin tingles
And the whole world's cheering!
    Then Ms. Downs repeats
        the question. . .
And—blang!—she's back,
    sitting, red-faced,
In Sixth Grade Social Studies,
Grabbing for the aftertrail
        of words.
And she answers, "Kenya?"

ISABEL JOSHLIN GLASER

JAIME'S WISH

I want to be a ballerina,
   Spinning on my toes.
I want to dance out on a stage
   With people clapping all in rows.

So I leap across the living room.
   I twirl around in circles.
I practice wearing floating gowns
   Of reds and pinks and purples.

I'd like to be a ballerina.
   And if I had the chance,
I know that I could be the best—
   If only I could dance.

CYNTHIA S. PEDERSON

THUMBPRINT

In the heel of my thumb
are whorls, whirls, wheels
in a unique design:
mine alone.
What a treasure to own!
My own flesh, my own feelings
No other, however grand or base,
can ever contain the same.
My signature,
thumbing the pages of my time.
My universe key,
my singularity.
Impress, implant,
I am myself,
of all my atom parts I am the sum.
And out of my blood and my brain
I make my own interior weather,
my own sun and rain.
Imprint my mark upon the world,
whatever I shall become.

EVE MERRIAM